Written by Emily Gale

Illustrated by Mark Marshall

This edition published by Parragon in 2010
Parragon
Queen Street House
4 Queen Street
Bath BA1 1HE, UK

ISBN 978-1-4454-0792-0

Printed in China

Doctor Pig

PaRragon

Bath · New York · Singapore · Hong Kong · Cologne · Delhi · Melbourne

Finley Pig was happy.

"Ahhhh!"

Life couldn't be better.

"It's alright for some!" said Agatha Chicken who was always sticking her beak in. "This is a busy farm, Lazybones," she clucked.

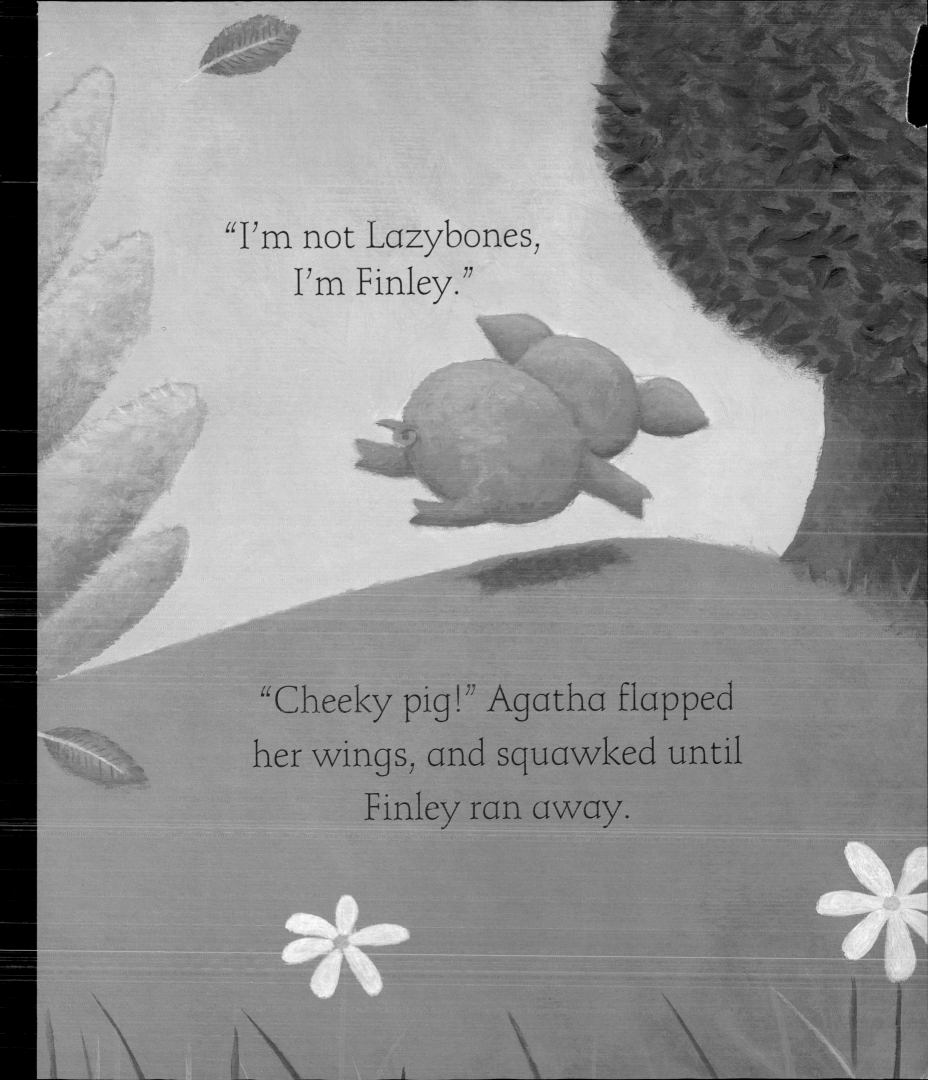

"I'm not Lazybones,
I'm Finley."

"Cheeky pig!" Agatha flapped
her wings, and squawked until
Finley ran away.

Finley sat under a tree to think.
Mud baths were lovely, but he did want
to be a big help on the busy farm.
What would he be good at?

"I've got it!"

Mommy Pig was puzzled.
"Where are you going with all that, Finley?"

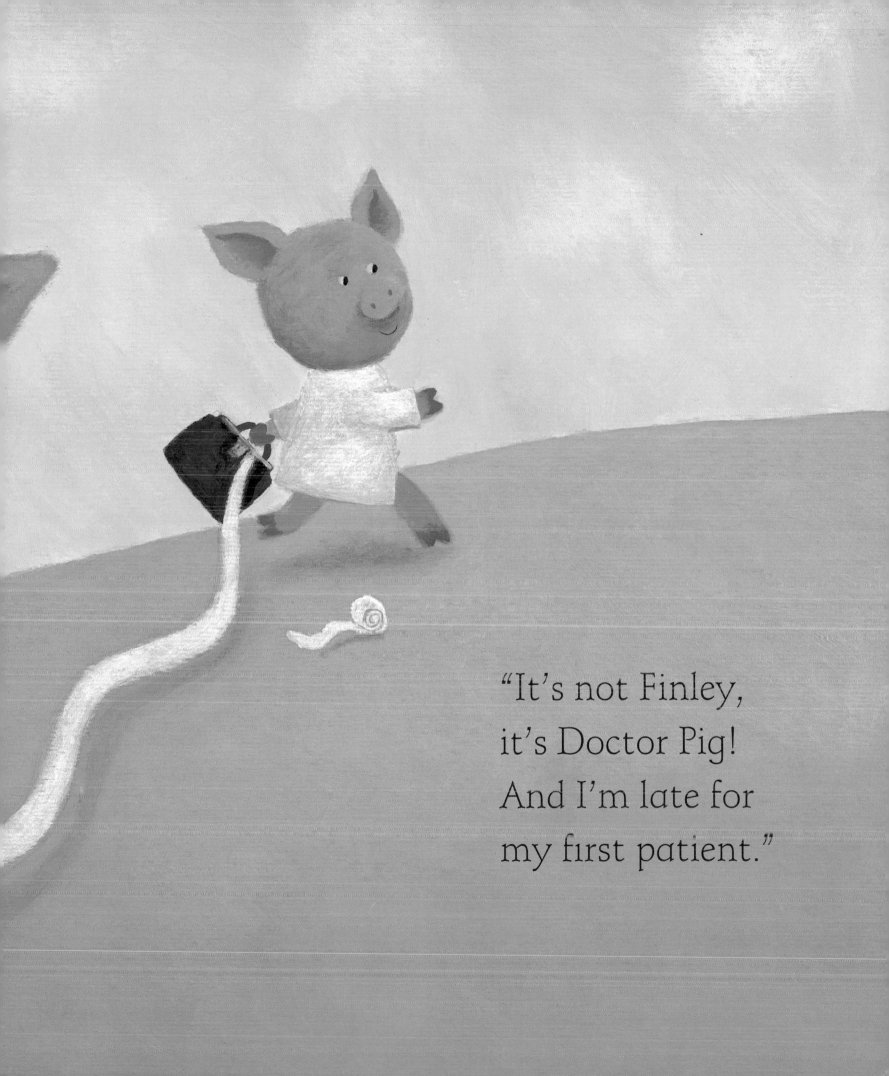

"It's not Finley,
it's Doctor Pig!
And I'm late for
my first patient."

"What seems to be the trouble, Mrs. Moo?"

Mrs. Moo moo'd.

"Don't say moo, say ahhh!" said Finley.

"Finley, there's nothing wrong with my leg."

"Hold still for Doctor Pig, please!"

Chester Sheep was not good at having his heart listened to—he wouldn't stop munching.

The geese, Heidi and Dora,
refused their medicine.

The sheepdog . . . ran away.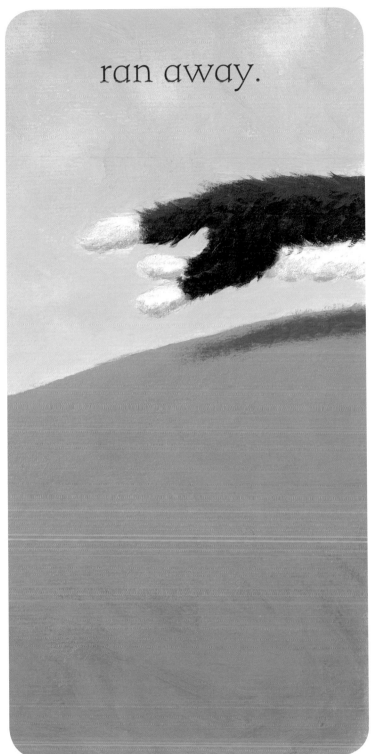

Being a doctor was really hard work, but the most difficult patients of all were . . .

. . . the
chickens.

At the end of a long day, Mommy Pig was pleased to see Finley.

"I'm very good at being a doctor," said Finley. "But I'm . . .

" . . . even better at being me.

Do Not Disturb

Ahhhh!"

Life couldn't be better.